African Adventure

KINGFISHER
LONDON & NEW YORK

Text copyright © Tony Mitton 2009
Illustrations copyright © Ant Parker 2009
Consultancy by David Burnie

Published in the United States by Kingfisher,
175 Fifth Ave., New York, NY 10010
Kingfisher is an imprint of Pan Macmillan, London.
All rights reserved.

Distributed in the U.S. and Canada by Macmillan, 175 Fifth Ave., New York, NY 10010

Library of Congress Cataloging-in-Publication Data
has been applied for.

ISBN: 978-0-7534-7230-9

Kingfisher books are available for special promotions and premiums. For details contact:
Special Markets Department, Macmillan, 175 Fifth Avenue, New York, NY 10010.

For more information, please visit www.kingfisherbooks.com

Printed in China
9 8 7 6 5 4 3 2 1
1TR/0115/LF/UTD/135MA

To Lauren Austin next door.
With best wishes—T. M.
For Bruno and Polar Cub—A. P.

African Adventure

Tony Mitton and Ant Parker

KINGFISHER
NEW YORK

In Africa the grassy plains
are vast and dry and hot.

They're teeming with wild animals.
There really are a lot!

Here's a herd of elephants.
They're bulky, big, and gray.

And yet they seem so gentle
as they wander on their way.

A happy hippopotamus
lies lolling in a pool.

The mud and water keep its skin
so smooth and moist and cool.

The zebra and the antelope
seem peaceful side by side.

Yet as they graze they're wary
of the nearby lion pride.

The lions look so scary.
They hunt to get their meat.

But only when they're hungry
and they need some food to eat.

A group of tall giraffes are browsing,
heads up in the sky.

Their long necks reach the treetops,
where luscious leaves grow high.

Rhinoceros have two tough horns
and skin that's very thick.

If they start to charge you,
you'd better back off-quick!

The cheetah chases antelope.
It's spotted, lean, and fast.

No creature sprints as swiftly.
Just see it speeding past.

Baboon troops go out foraging
for tasty grassland snacks.

The little babies ride upon their busy parents' backs.

We've seen some grassland creatures
on our trip across the plain.

You might just spot some others
if you make the trip again.

Did you see . . .

the leopard?

the kori bustard?

the wildebeest?

the vulture?

the meerkats?

the crocodile?

the ostrich?

the oxpeckers?

the wart hogs?